JACK AND THE BEANSTALK

FULL-COLOR PICTURE BOOK
by J. Sainsbury's Pure Tea

DOVER PUBLICATIONS, INC.
NEW YORK

ONCE UPON A TIME there lived a poor widow and her son Jack. One day, to pay the bills, the poor widow decided she would have to sell their cow. She gave it to Jack and told him to take it to the town market, where he could sell it. "And make sure you get a good price," she warned Jack.

On the road to the market, Jack met a man who offered to buy the cow for a handful of beans. The beans, claimed the stranger, were magic. Jack took the beans and gave the man the cow.

Jack went home and told his mother about the beans. She was very angry, for she did not think the beans were magic. She threw the beans out of the window and sent Jack to bed without his supper.

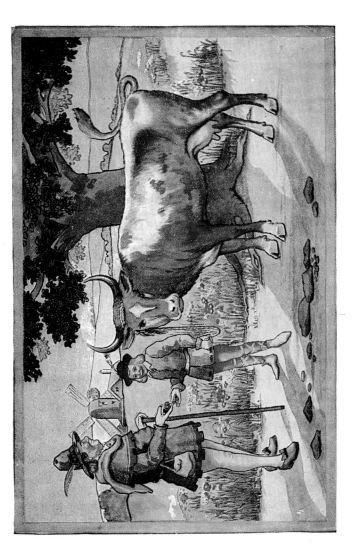

When Jack woke up next morning, he found that the beans had sprouted during the night, and a huge beanstalk had grown outside his window. It reached up into the clouds. Jack was an adventurous lad, and decided to climb the beanstalk. When he got to the top, he saw a country in the clouds, and a great castle in the distance.

Nearby stood a fairy, who told him that an evil giant lived in the castle. The giant had a treasure of gold coins, a hen that laid golden eggs and a harp that sang by itself— all of which the giant had stolen from Jack's father years earlier.

Jack knocked on the door, which was opened by the giant's wife. "Good morning," he said. "I wonder if you would give me something to eat." "Quick, boy," she cried, "get away from here! Don't you know my husband is a giant who likes nothing better than eating little boys like you?" Even as she spoke, the ground shook as the giant approached.

The giant's wife hid Jack in the oven just as the giant opened the door and walked in. He sniffed the air and said,

"FEE-FI-FO-FUM,
I smell the blood of an Englishman.
Be he alive, or be he dead,
I'll use his bones to grind my bread."

"But there's no one here," said his wife.

The giant ate his supper and took out his sacks of golden coins, which he began to count. Then he became drowsy and fell asleep. Jack rushed out, grabbed the sacks and took them with him down the beanstalk to his mother.

The next day, Jack climbed back up the beanstalk and hid himself in the giant's castle. Once again the giant came in and said,

**"FEE-FI-FO-FUM,
I smell the blood of an Englishman!"**

"Nonsense, dear," said his wife. "Sit down and have your nice game pie." When the giant had finished, he brought out his hen.

"Lay, hen," commanded the giant. And the hen laid one golden egg after another.

The giant grew drowsy and fell asleep. Jack rushed out, grabbed the hen and brought it down the beanstalk to his mother.

The next day, Jack once again climbed the beanstalk and hid himself in the giant's castle. The giant entered and said,

"FEE-FI-FO-FUM,
I smell the blood of an Englishman!"

But his wife assured him there was no one there and served him his supper.

When the giant had finished his supper, he called for his harp. The harp was set on the table and began to sing. Soon the giant fell asleep to the harp's song.

Jack slipped out of his hiding place and snatched the harp. But as he was running off with the harp, the harp cried out, "Help, master!" The giant awoke immediately and ran after Jack. Jack managed to keep ahead of the giant.

Jack ran to the beanstalk and climbed down as fast as he could, the giant right behind him. Jack reached the ground before the giant and ran into his house.

Jack grabbed an ax, rushed back to the beanstalk and began to chop away at it. He chopped and he chopped till he had chopped it right through. Then the beanstalk came tumbling down, the giant with it. He landed with a tremendous crash and was killed at once.

Jack and his mother kept the gold, the hen and the harp, and lived happily ever after.